Bear Up
A Child Learns to Handle
Ups and Downs

"I have learned to be content whatever the circumstances."
Philippians 4:11

To be happy, children and adults all finally have to learn how to cope with the ups and downs of life — the disappointments and minor frustrations of everyday living. *Bear Up* will help you teach your children some of these important and valuable coping skills.

A BEAR HUGS BOOK ™

Love Bears All Things: A Child Learns to Love

Bear Up: A Child Learns to Handle Ups and Downs

Bearing Burdens: A Child Learns to Help

Bear Buddies: A Child Learns to Make Friends

Bearing Fruit: A Child Learns About the Fruit of the Spirit

I Can Bearly Wait: A Child Learns Patience

Titles in Preparation:

Bears Repeating: A Child Learns Thankfulness

You are Beary Special: A Child Learns Self-esteem

Bear Necessities: A Child Learns Obedience

Bear Facts: A Child Learns Truthfulness

Bearing Good News: A Child Learns to Be Positive

Sweeter Than Honey: A Child Learns the Golden Rule

Copyright 1986, Paul C. Brownlow
Hardcover, ISBN: 0-915720-51-5
Library Edition, ISBN: 0-915720-60-4

Brownlow Publishing Company, Inc.
6309 Airport Freeway, Fort Worth, Texas 76117

Bear Up
A Child Learns to Handle Ups and Downs

By

Pat Kirk & Alice Brown

Illustrated by

Diann Bartnick

BROWNLOW PUBLISHING COMPANY, INC.

Life has its ups and downs!
How we love the ups.

But life can also have its downs.
They can make us want to frown.

Life's not a tough hill for this bear
to climb. He's learned to be happy
most of the time.

Say, "Hi," to Bear Able and
"How do you do!" He can make
your life bearable, too!

Able knows the sun can't always stay.

So he makes the best of a rainy day.

Bear Able has a party in his heart
even when the party never starts.

He can still find a way
to celebrate his special day.

Bear Able may not get to go
to every party or picture show.

But he doesn't get excited when
others, not him, all get invited.

Able can bear it when
all the fun goes flat.

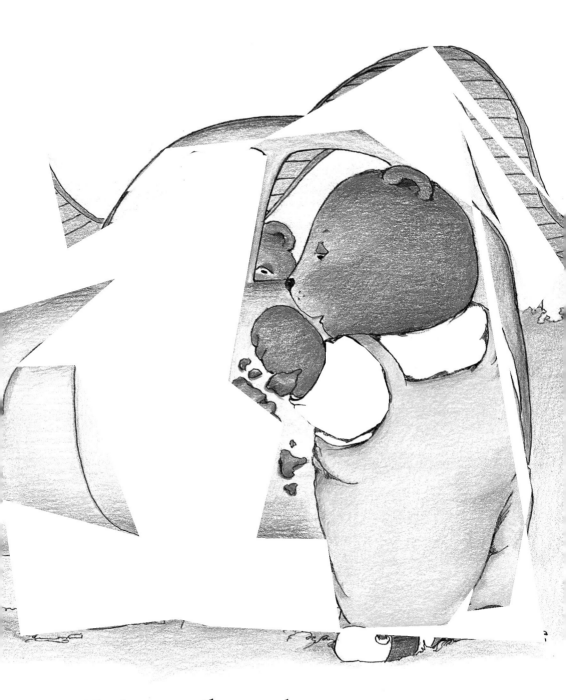

He just smiles and says,
"Well, I guess that's that."

Bear Able goes to the dentist
and doctor cheerfully.

He knows these helpers
are his friends, you see.

Screaming and jumping

don't help wounds heal.

So Bear Able relaxes,

stays calm and still.

When Able makes a mistake
at home or during school,

he doesn't try to hide it
    by acting really "cool."

Bear Able always asks himself,
"What will happen if I do this or that?"

And Able saves himself from
many a tumble and many a splat.

Able is happy to help

little bears get across.

He shows them he cares.

He doesn't bully or boss.

Bear Able says kind words so
he never has to bear shame

when someone tells what
he said and uses his name.

When it's time to stop playing,

Able doesn't cry or make a big fuss.
He just puts up his paints
and cleans up his brush.

Let's be like Bear Able.

He climbs the hills up and down.
He's learned how to be happy
and he's so nice to be around.

God made us all with feelings.
We're not puppets with strings.
But God can use our feelings
to give our lives wings.

So give God your ups
and give him your downs.
He'll use them to make you
the best you around!